Next Please

Ernst Jandl and Norman Junge

Text © Hermann Luchterhand Verlag GmbH & Co KG, Darmstadt and Neuwied 1970.
First published in Germany by Luchterhand Literaturverlag, Munich in 1970.
Translation © Hutchinson Children's Books 2001.
fünfter sein © Beltz Verlag, Weinham and Basel 1997.
Programm Beltz & Gelberg, Weinheim.
First published in the United Kingdom in 2001 by Hutchinson Children's Books.
by G. P. Putnam's Sons, a division of Penguin Putnam Books for Young Readers,
345 Hudson Street, New York, NY 10014.
G. P. Putnam's Sons, Reg. U.S. Pat. & Tm. Off.
Printed in Hing Kong. Text set in Cochin.
Library of Congress Cataloging-in-Publication Data
Jandl, Ernst, 1925– [Fünfter sein. English]
Next please / Ernst Jandl; illustrated by Norman Junge.— 1st American ed.
p.   cm. Summary: One by one, injured toys are called from the waiting room
and sent out as good as new, until only the fifth one is left.
[1. Wounds and injuries—Fiction. 2. Patience—Fiction. 3. Toys—Fiction.]
I. Junge, Norman, ill. II. Title. PZ7.J19 Ne 2002 [E]—dc21 00-069687
ISBN 0-399-23758-5
1 3 5 7 9 10 8 6 4 2
First Impression

Next Please

Ernst Jandl and Norman Junge

G. P. Putnam's Sons   New York

Five are waiting.

Door opens.
One comes out.

"Next, please."
One goes in.

Four waiting.

Door opens.
One comes out.

"Next, please."
One goes in.

Three waiting.

Door opens.
One comes out.

"Next, please."
One goes in.

Two waiting.

Door opens.
One comes out.

"Next, please."
One goes in.

One waiting.
All alone.

Door opens.
One comes out.

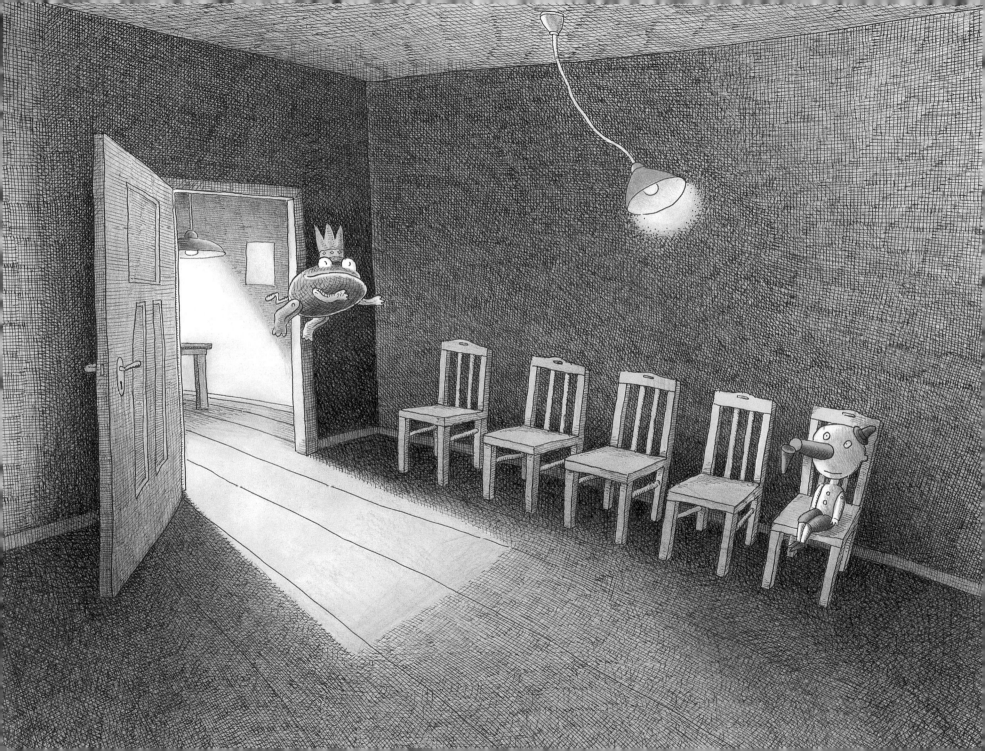

"Next, please."
Last one goes in.

"Hello, Doctor."
"Your nose again? Don't worry. I'll fix you right up."

None waiting.